CONSTRUCTION BALANCE

Lee-Anne Spalding

Bethany, Missouri

Photo Credits:
Cover, Title Page © constructionphotographs.com; Pages 5, 9, 17, 19 © pirpower.com; Pages 7, 8, 11, 13, 14,
21, 22 © constructionphotographs.com; Page 15 © Frances Twitty

Cataloging-in-Publication Data

Spalding, Lee-Anne
    Construction balance / Lee-Anne Spalding. — 1st ed.
    p. cm. — (Construction zone science)

    Includes bibliographical references and index.
    Summary: Series offers text and photographs to
introduce science concepts as found at construction sites.
    ISBN-13: 978-1-4242-1381-8 (lib. bdg. : alk. paper)
    ISBN-10: 1-4242-1381-9 (lib. bdg. : alk. paper)
    ISBN-13: 978-1-4242-1471-6 (pbk. : alk. paper)
    ISBN-10: 1-4242-1471-8 (pbk. : alk. paper)

    1. Levers—Juvenile literature. 2. Mechanical movements—
Juvenile literature. 3. Equilibrium—Juvenile literature.
4. Stability—Juvenile literature.
5. Building sites—Juvenile literature. [1. Levers.
2. Mechanical movements. 3. Equilibrium. 4. Building sites.
5. Motion.] I. Spalding, Lee-Anne. II. Title.
III. Series.
    TJ147.S63 2007
    531'.3—dc22

First edition
© 2007 Fitzgerald Books
802 N. 41st Street, P.O. Box 505
Bethany, MO 64424, U.S.A.
Printed in China
Library of Congress Control Number: 2006940864

TABLE OF CONTENTS

BALANCE?

Balance at a **construction site** is important. Balance means a condition in which opposing forces are equal to each other.

On the job site, workers **construct** buildings and balance things like wood, so they do not fall down.

MACHINES BALANCE

Machines need to balance. This truck uses extra support to balance. When something on a job site is balanced, it is also stable. Stable things make a safer construction site.

Balance Support

CRANES BALANCE

Workers use a machine called a crane to lift heavy **loads**. The arm of the crane uses a cable to lift the loads. For the crane to work, the loads must balance!

Cable

Load

9

FORKLIFTS BALANCE

Like the crane, a forklift also carries heavy loads. The load balances on the two arms of the forklift. The load can then be lifted up and down.

Arms

Load

TOOLS BALANCE

Workers need tools on a construction site. **Sawhorses** and **tripods** help workers build. Two sawhorses balance wood for sawing. Tripods, balancing on three legs, hold instruments that measure the land.

Tripod

LADDERS BALANCE

Like sawhorses and tripods, ladders are helpful tools. Ladders help workers reach higher places. Some tall ladders balance by leaning against buildings.

WORKERS BALANCE

Workers need to balance just like their machines and tools. Workers balance on a **scaffold** to build on a construction site. The scaffold supports them and helps them reach higher places.

Scaffold

BODIES BALANCE

Workers' bodies must balance to keep them safe! When working in high places, on beams and roofs, workers must balance to do their jobs.

If balance is lost, workers could get hurt!

HELP TO BALANCE

Sometimes workers wear **harnesses**. If a worker loses his balance, the harness keeps him from falling down. The harness keeps the worker safe on a construction site!

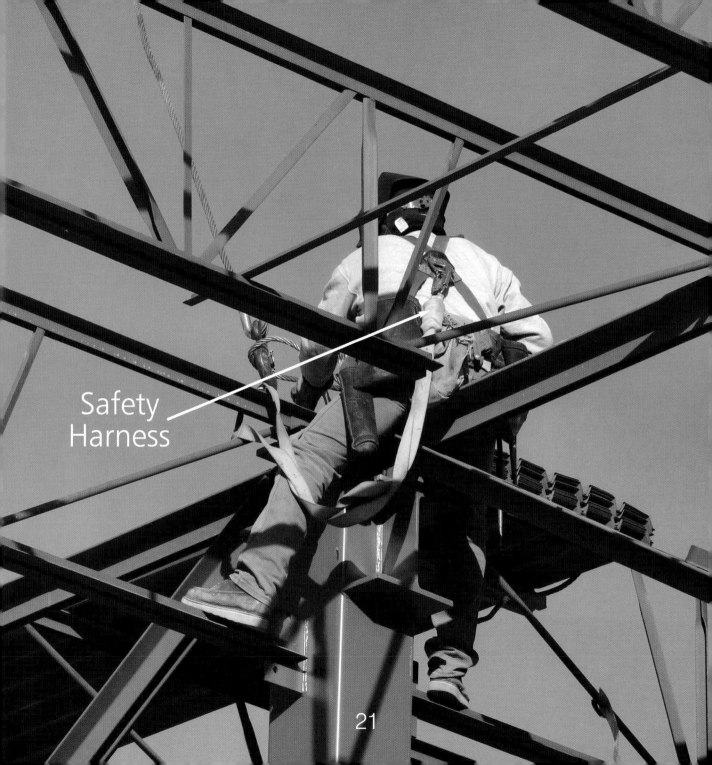

Safety
Harness

SUMMARY

Machines, tools, and even workers need to balance on the construction site. Balance allows machines and tools to work properly. Keeping their balance helps workers stay safe on the job!

GLOSSARY

construct (kuhn STRUHKT) — to build

construction site (kuhn STRUHKT shun SITE) — a place where workers build

harness (HAR niss) — straps and fastenings that support something or someone

load (LOHD) — something that is carried

machine (muh SHEEN) — something that uses energy to help people work

sawhorse (SAW hors) — a frame on which wood is laid for sawing

scaffold (SKAF old) — a supporting framework

tripod (TRYE pod) — a three-legged stand

INDEX

FURTHER READING

C Is for Construction: Big Trucks and Diggers from A to Z. Chronicle Books, 2003.
Pallotta, Jerry. *The Construction Alphabet Book.* Charlesbridge Publishers, 2006.

WEBSITES TO VISIT

Because Internet links change so often, Fitzgerald Books has developed an online list of websites related to the subject of this book. This site is updated regularly. Please use this link to access the list: www.fitzgeraldbookslinks.com/czs/cb

ABOUT THE AUTHOR

Lee-Anne Trimble Spalding is a former public school educator and is currently instructing preservice teachers at the University of Central Florida. She lives in Oviedo, Florida with her husband, Brett, and two sons, Graham and Gavin.